CHORES

To order additional copies of this book, contact:
Xlibris
844-714-8691
www.Xlibris.com
Orders@Xlibris.com

ISBN: Softcover   978-1-6698-7177-4
       EBook   978-1-6698-7178-1

Print information available on the last page

Rev. date: 04/04/2023

THE ADVENTURES OF KEVEN'S WORLD

CHORES

WRITTEN BY: KEVEN PUGH

ILLUSTRATED BY: JOSHUA BONNEAU

Keven picks up his toys and begins to put them away.

Afterwards, he met his dad in the kitchen. Dad showed Keven how to wash dishes.

One week went by and keven did all his chores.

Dad looks around with a big smile on his face.

14

Keven continued doing his chores and assisting Mrs. Johnson with her trash.

Another week had passed, Dad gave Keven his $20 and Mrs. Johnson gave Keven $10.

Keven is able to invest, save and spend with the money he earned doing his chores.

"And This is Keven's World"

KEVEN'S WORLD

Scan the QR Code for the full
Keven's World experience!!!